Contents

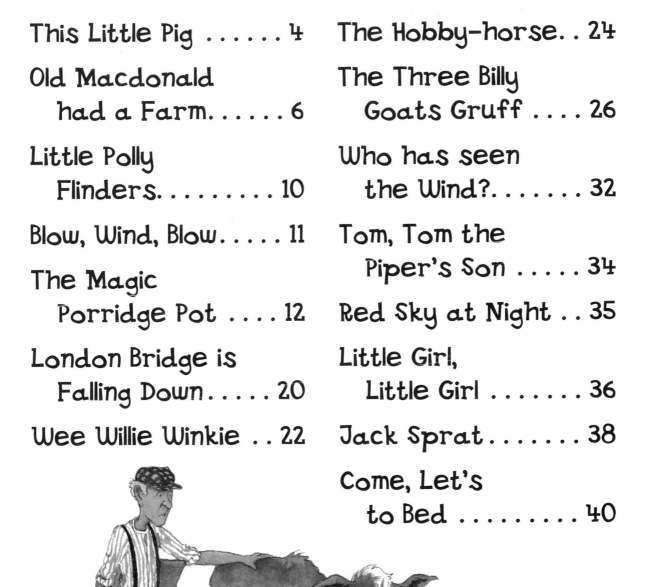

This Little Pig

This little pig went to market,
This little pig stayed at home,
This little pig had roast beef,
This little pig had none,

*Read the first line
and wiggle the big toe.*

*Read the next line
and wiggle the next
toe and so on...*

*On the final line
tickle the foot.*

And this little pig cried,
"Wee-wee-wee-wee-wee!"
All the way home.

Old Macdonald had a Farm

Old Macdonald had a farm,
E-I-E-I-O!
And on that farm he had some cows,
E-I-E-I-O!

With a moo-moo here,
And a moo-moo there,
Here a moo, there a moo,
everywhere a moo-moo,
Old Macdonald had a farm,
E-I-E-I-O!

Old Macdonald had a farm,
E-I-E-I-O!
And on that farm he had some sheep,
E-I-E-I-O!

With a baa-baa here,
And a baa-baa there,
Here a baa, there a baa,
everywhere a baa-baa,
Old Macdonald had a farm,
E-I-E-I-O!

Old Macdonald had a farm,
E-I-E-I-O!
And on that farm he had some ducks,
E-I-E-I-O!

With a quack-quack here,
And a quack-quack there,
Here a quack, there a quack,
everywhere a quack-quack,
Old Macdonald had a farm,
E-I-E-I-O!

Old Macdonald had a farm,
E-I-E-I-O!
And on that farm he had some pigs,
E-I-E-I-O!

With an oink-oink here,
And an oink-oink there,
Here an oink, there an oink,
everywhere an oink-oink,
Old Macdonald had a farm,
E-I-E-I-O!

Little Polly Flinders

Little Polly Flinders
Sat among the cinders,
Warming her pretty little toes.

Her mother came and
caught her,
And scolded her
Dear daughter,
For spoiling her
Nice new clothes.

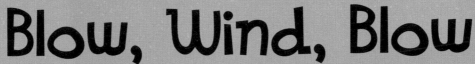
Blow, Wind, Blow

Blow, wind, blow, and go, mill, go,
That the miller may grind his corn;
That the baker may take it,
And into bread make it,
And bring us a loaf in the morn.

The Magic Porridge Pot

A Swedish folk tale

One day, just before Christmas, a poor old farmer and his wife decided that they needed to sell their last cow. They had no money left and no food in the cupboard. As the farmer walked sadly to market with the cow, he met a very strange little man on the way. He had a long white beard right down to his toes, which were bare, and he wore a huge black hat, under which the farmer could only just see the bright gleam of his eyes. Over his arm he carried a battered old porridge pot.

"That's a nice looking cow," said the little man. "Is she for sale?"

"Yes," said the farmer.

"I shall buy your cow," declared the little man, putting the porridge pot down with a thump. "I shall give you this porridge pot in exchange for your cow!"

Well, the farmer looked at the battered old porridge pot, and he looked at his fine cow. And he was just about to say, "Certainly not!" when a voice whispered, "Take me! Take me!"

The farmer shook himself. Dear me, it was bad enough to be poor without beginning to hear strange voices. He opened his mouth again to say, "Certainly not!" when he heard the voice again. "Take me! Take me!"

Well, he saw at once that it must be a magic pot, and he knew you didn't hang about with magic pots, so he said very quickly to the little man, "Certainly!" and handed over the cow. He bent down to pick up the pot, and when he looked up, the little man had vanished.

The farmer knew he was going to have a difficult time explaining to his wife just how he had come to part with their precious cow for a battered old porridge pot.

She was very angry indeed and had started to say a lot of very cross things when a voice came from the pot,

"Take me inside and clean me and polish me, and you shall see what you shall see!"

Well, the farmer's wife was astonished but she did as she was bid. She washed the pot inside and out, and then she polished it until it shone as bright as a new pin. No sooner had she finished than the pot hopped off the table, and out of the door. The farmer and his wife sat down by the fire, not saying a word to each other. They had no money, no cow, no food and now it seemed they didn't even have their magic pot.

Down the road from the poor farmer, there lived a rich man. He was very selfish and spent all his time eating huge meals and counting his money. He had lots of servants, including a cook who was in the kitchen making a Christmas pudding. The pudding was stuffed with plums, currants, sultanas, almonds and goodness knows what else. It was so big that the cook realized she didn't have a pot to boil it in. It was at this point that the porridge pot trotted in the door.

"Goodness me!" she exclaimed. "The fairies must have sent this pot just in time to take my pudding," and she dropped the pudding in the pot. No sooner had the pudding fallen to the bottom with a very satisfying thud, than the pot skipped out of the door again. The cook gave a great shriek, but by the time the butler and the footman and the parlour maid and the boy who turned the spit had all dashed into the kitchen, the pot was quite out of sight.

The porridge pot in the meantime trotted down the road to the poor farmer's house. He and his wife were delighted to see the pot again, and even more pleased when they discovered the wonderful pudding. The wife boiled it up and it lasted them for three days. So they had a good Christmas after all, while the porridge pot sat by the fire.

Spring came, and still the porridge pot sat quietly by the fire. Then one day the pot suddenly trotted over to the farmer's wife and said, "Clean me, and polish me, and you shall see what you shall see."

So the farmer's wife polished the pot till it shone as bright as a new pin.

No sooner had she finished than the pot hopped off the table, and out of the door.

You will remember that the rich man was very fond of counting his money. There he sat in the great hall, with piles of golden guineas and silver sixpences on the table, and great bulging bags of coins on the floor at his feet. He was wondering where he could hide the money when in trotted the pot. Now the cook had been far too frightened of the rich man's temper to tell him about the pot stealing the Christmas pudding, so when he saw the pot he was delighted.

"Goodness me!" he exclaimed, "The fairies must have sent this pot just in time to take my money," and he dropped several bags of money in the pot. No sooner had the bags fallen to the bottom with a very satisfying clink, than the pot skipped out of the door again. The rich man shouted and hollered, but by the time the coachman and the head groom and the stable lad had run into the great hall, the pot was quite out of sight.

It trotted down the road to the poor farmer's house. He and his wife were delighted to see the pot again, and even more pleased when they discovered the bags of gold and silver. There was enough money to last them for the rest of their days, even after they had bought a new cow.

As for the battered old porridge pot, it sat by the fire for many a long year. Then, one day, it suddenly trotted straight out of the door. It went off up the road until it was out of sight, and the farmer and his wife never saw it again.

London Bridge is Falling Down

London Bridge is falling down,
Falling down, falling down,
London Bridge is falling down,
My fair lady.

Wee Willie Winkie

Wee Willie Winkie
Runs through the town,
Upstairs and downstairs
In his nightgown,

Rapping at the window,
Crying through the lock,
"Are the children in their beds,
For now it's eight o'clock?"

23

The Hobby-horse

I had a little hobby-horse,
And it was dapple grey;
Its head was made of pea-straw,
Its tail was made of hay.

I sold it to an old woman
For a copper groat;
And I'll not sing my song again
Without another coat.

The Three Billy Goats Gruff

A folk tale from Europe

In a mountain valley beside a rushing river, there lived three billy goats. One was very small, one was middle-sized and one was huge, and they were called the Three Billy Goats Gruff. Every day they would eat the lush green grass by the river, and they were very content.

One day, however, the Three Billy Goats Gruff decided they would like to cross the river and see if the grass was any greener on the other side. The grass was actually no greener, nor was it any tastier, but they all felt they would like a change. First they had to find a way to cross the rushing river. They trotted a good way upstream before they found a little wooden bridge. After a supper of lush green grass, they decided to wait until next morning before crossing the wooden bridge, so they settled down for the night.

Now, what the Three Billy Goats Gruff did not know was that under the little wooden bridge there lived an extremely mean and grumpy troll. He could smell the

Three Billy Goats Gruff, and he thought they smelled good enough to eat. So the next morning when the Three Billy Goats Gruff had eaten a breakfast of lush green grass, the troll was hiding under the little wooden bridge, waiting for his chance to have breakfast too.

"That little wooden bridge does not look too strong," said the very small Billy Goat Gruff. "I will go across first to see if it is safe," and he trotted across the little wooden bridge. But when he was only halfway across, the mean and grumpy troll leapt out of his hiding place.

"Who is that trit-trotting across my bridge?" he roared. "I am going to eat you up!"

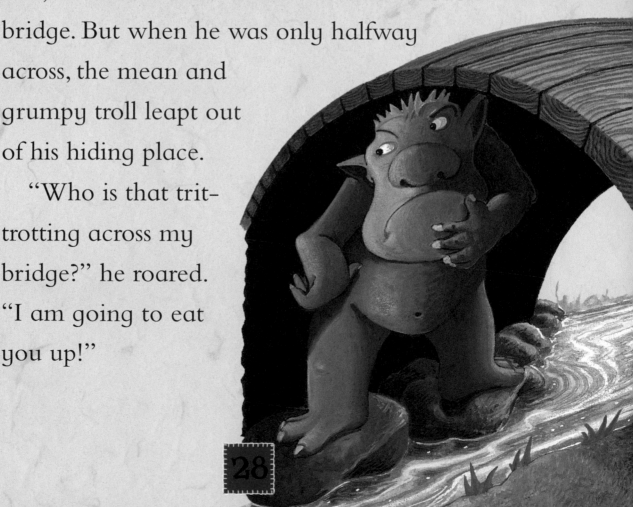

But the very small Billy Goat Gruff wasn't ready to be eaten up just yet, so he bravely said to the mean and grumpy troll, "You don't want to eat a skinny, bony thing like me. Just wait till my brother comes across, he is much bigger," and with a skip and a hop, the very small Billy Goat Gruff ran across the bridge to the lush green grass on the other side.

The middle-sized Billy Goat Gruff started to cross the little wooden bridge, but when he was only halfway across, the mean and grumpy troll roared at him.

"Who is that trit-trotting across my bridge?" he roared. "I am going to eat you up!"

But the middle-sized Billy Goat Gruff wasn't ready to be eaten up just yet either, so he bravely said to the mean and grumpy troll, "You don't want to eat a skinny, bony thing like me. Wait till my brother comes across, he is even bigger," and with a skip and a hop, the middle-sized Billy Goat Gruff ran across the bridge to the lush green grass on the other side.

Now, the huge Billy Goat Gruff had been watching all the time. He smiled to himself and stepped onto the little wooden bridge. By this time the troll was very hungry, and he was even meaner and grumpier when he was hungry. He didn't bother to hide, but stood in the middle of

the bridge looking at the huge Billy Goat Gruff who came trotting up to him.

"Who is that trit-trotting across my bridge?" he roared for a third time. "I am going to eat you up!"

"Oh no, you won't!" said the huge Billy Goat Gruff, and he lowered his head and with his huge horns he biffed the mean and grumpy troll into the rushing river. The water carried him far away down the river, and he was never seen again. The Three Billy Goats Gruff lived happily for many more years eating the lush green grass, and they were able to cross the river whenever they wanted!

Who has seen the Wind?

Who has seen the wind?
Neither I nor you;
But when the leaves hang trembling,
The wind is passing through.

Who has seen the wind?
Neither you nor I;
But when the trees bow down
their heads,
The wind is passing by.

Christina Rossetti
1830–94, b. England

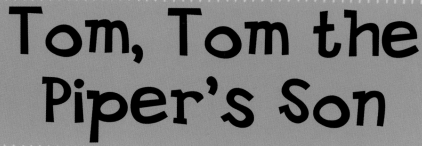

Tom, Tom the Piper's Son

Tom, Tom the piper's son,
Stole a pig and away he run,
The pig was eat,
And Tom was beat,
And Tom went howling
Down the street.

Red Sky at Night

Red sky at night,
Shepherd's delight;
Red sky in the morning,
Shepherd's warning.

Little Girl, Little Girl

Little girl, little girl,
Where have you been?
Gathering roses to give
To the queen.

Little girl, little girl,
What gave she you?
She gave me a
Diamond as big
As my shoe.

37

Jack Sprat

Jack Sprat could eat no fat,
His wife could eat no lean,
So between them both,
you see,
They licked the
platter clean.

Jack ate all the lean,
Joan ate all the fat,
The bone they picked it clean,
Then gave it to the cat.

Come, Let's to Bed

Come, let's to bed, says Sleepy-head;
Sit up awhile, says Slow;
Bang on the pot, says Greedy-gut,
We'll sup before we go.

To bed, to bed, cried Sleepy-head,
But all the rest said No!
It is morning now,
You must milk the cow,
And tomorrow to bed we go.